ELVIS AND THE

STONE

PHILOSOPHERS

KRAMER WOLF

For Joe, with love

CONTENTS

1. THE LAST LAUGH

Elvis didn't like the look of it. He'd been at the Academy for almost a year, and nothing like this had happened before.

As he took his seat in the Great Hall he noticed with some alarm that his hands were trembling, and a prickly sweat was gathering beneath the dark fringe of his forehead. Not since they had come for him, taking him from his parents' house in the middle of the night – not since that evil time had he known such a sense of utter dread.

The others were sensing it too; he could see it in their eyes as, one by one, they took their seats. All of them, like him, had been taken from their families and friends over the past year, to study at the Academy. None had been given any say in the matter.

Because on Planet Stone ... *Walton Flowers was God.*

The lights were dimming and the packed-out hall fell into silence as a single spotlight illuminated the stage. Elvis sat in the midst of the silent crowd, his mind racing over the events of the last hour. He had been in the dormitory with his three best friends when the voice had broken through the speakers.

"Would all students make their way immediately to the Great Hall for the Extraordinary Meeting."

George had looked up with a puzzled expression. *Extraordinary Meeting* - what's that about?"

"Whatever it is," said Elvis, "I don't like the sound of it."

"I've never been inside the Great Hall," said John.

"Lucky you," said Elvis.

"Why do you say that?" asked Ryan.

Elvis shrugged. "Things I've heard, that's all."

The other three boys were staring at him, waiting to hear what he knew.

At last Elvis gave in to their impatience stares. "It's just that – well, I've heard that the hall is only ever used for ... *meetings*."

"What kind of meetings?" asked George.

"Extraordinary Meetings."

"Look," said John. "If you know something, tells us."

"I don't know much."

"I think you know enough," said Ryan. "What is it?"

"It's these meetings," said Elvis. "They mean something's going to happen. Something - well - something massive. They call people from all over the planet and they make laws."

"But we've never been called to one of these meetings before," said George.

"That's what's bothering me," said Elvis. "The law makers aren't teenagers like us. They're adults. I think this has to do with all the jokes we've been telling."

"What are you talking about?" asked John.

"Jokes?" said Ryan. "Who've you been talking to?"

But Elvis hadn't been talking to anybody. He'd been too busy listening, watching, and reading between the lines. He'd been too busy sensing that something awful was coming, and coming in the shape of the Fat Professor.

A steady drum beat shook the silence in the Great Hall and a familiar figure filled the stage.

Professor Walton Flowers was easy on neither the eye nor the ear. Even at a distance he gave the impression, not of flesh, blood and bone, but of rubber. And not just any old rubber: loud, in-your-face rubber that has been dangerously over-inflated.

To catch him straight on, his shape was roughly that of a diamond, with a smallish head and surprisingly small feet; yet with a waist that only a fool would think of walking around without a packed lunch and ample supplies of water.

His voice kicked in.

And it was angry.

Walton Flowers was always angry, except when he was trying to tell awful jokes that nobody laughed at.

And people not laughing at his jokes was the thing that made him angriest of all.

It was a strange thing that Elvis had noticed from the very beginning: that when the Fat Professor was angry he could be funny. And when he was steaming with anger he could be hilarious. Yet when he was angry was just the time when you were *not* supposed to laugh at him. And if you did it made him even angrier.

And therefore funnier.

Yet when he was trying to be funny, telling the worst jokes ever, he wasn't the least bit funny and nobody ever felt the least like laughing.

Which made him angry.

Which in turn made him funnier still.

It was a paradox. And being a philosopher, Elvis loved a paradox, particularly a funny one.

"I have called this meeting because there is some serious business to attend to."

The anger in the Fat Professor's voice made Elvis wonder if he hadn't been telling jokes again, and nobody laughing.

Despite the sense of dread Elvis felt the beginnings of a smile forming. He just couldn't help it.

" ... In a moment you will all witness an event, here in this hall, that none of you will ever forget. This is a day that will be talked about for generations to come; a day on which history is to be made; a day long overdue."

The Fat Professor's voice was exploding around the Great Hall like so many bombs, yet the pompous tone had Elvis biting his lip to stop him from breaking out into a full-blown grin.

"In the course of my studies, which have been long and considerable, I have become aware of a plague that is destroying this great world in which we live. Yes, a plague, here, on Stone - the jewel of the universe. And I have located this plague and mean to wipe it from the face of our world, and will do so, in a moment."

He took something yellow from the pocket of his gigantic jacket.

A banana.

With great ceremony he began to peel the banana; and then, with considerably less ceremony, he wolfed the poor fruit down in one.

Elvis had a hand over his mouth, trying to hold back his laughter. The Fat Professor was clearly not playing this for laughs, and there was a simple enough way of establishing that: if he had been playing it for laughs, it would not have been the least bit funny.

"I now ask that my assistant join me on stage for the punch line."

For a moment the spotlight moved from Walton Flowers to a thin, weasel-faced man who looked suspiciously like an actor. Then the spotlight moved back to the Fat Professor as he held the banana skin above his head.

"What you are about to witness here today is my single-handed destruction of the plague that is destroying our world."

The anger in the fat voice was becoming brutal and Elvis could hardly stand it. Dread of what was coming had merged with the need to let out some serious laughter, and something was going to have to give.

"Laughter!"

Walton Flowers spat out the word.

"I say again: *Laughter!* That is the plague that Stone must fight against and destroy."

Then, in an instant, everything changed. The anger was gone, replaced by a look on the Fat Professor's face that Elvis knew all too well.

There was a joke coming.

"What you are about to witness is the Last Laugh. With the help of my able assistant I will provide you with a fitting end to laughter in this world. My finest joke: the finest joke that this world could ever know. And we will laugh together and put an end to laughter ... forever. Now: a drum roll if you please."

The drum rolled and Walton Flowers shared the spotlight as the actor walked towards him. Then Flowers threw down the banana skin and the actor stepped on to it before slipping, deliberately and dramatically, landing flat on his back as the drum roll climaxed. The Fat Professor turned to the audience to accept its final gift of laughter.

But nobody laughed. There was not so much as a smile on any of the faces of the Academy students.

It was the worst joke of all time.

The clock ticked and the silence in the hall deepened, becoming a thing of terror. The tensions inside Elvis were building dangerously, and as the Fat Professor's face clenched and glared with appalling anger in the wake of his failed joke, the young student thought he was about to burst.

The Fat Professor looked down on his assistant, who was still sitting next to the banana skin. "Well, are you planning on staying down there for the rest of your life? What kind of fool are you, ruining the finest joke that was ever conceived? Get up, man!"

The actor got up quickly before slinking off stage and leaving Walton Flowers to redirect his anger back out onto the crowd.

"Well, that was your last chance. From this moment on laughter is banned from this world."

Elvis was shaking from head to toe, holding back the desperate urge to laugh. Both hands were over his face when his body finally let him down.

And that's when something truly historic happened.

The awful silence was broken as the teenage philosophy genius let out a blast of wind that almost ripped his underpants clean in half.

The spotlight swung out over the gathering.

"That sounded to me like a fifteen-year-old fart," said the Fat Professor, sternly.

Now laughter ruptured the tattered remains of the deathly silence.

"By which I do not of course mean that the fart was fifteen years old, rather ... *silence!* Have I not just banished laughter from this world?"

The entire Academy was split in half: those laughing uncontrollably and those holding in the urge to laugh; yet with so much nervous tension in the air, something was bound to give.

Another blast ripped through the hall, then another, and yet another.

The spotlight was swinging furiously around the assembled students, trying to locate the offender, or offenders.

But the blasts were intensifying, one after another rifling the air like so much machine-gun fire. And with the cacophony of wind came more laughter, spreading through the Great Hall like the plague that Walton Flowers was so determined to wipe from the face of his world.

On the darkened stage, the Fat Professor stood alone in a self-contained cloud of fury that buzzed with the desire for retribution. He could see who – what – sat at the centre of this outrage.

It seemed that talent came at a price. That the most talented student this Academy had yet produced, was also its most dangerous.

The cacophony was dying down.

Walton Flowers waited.

A new silence grew and he let it. And only when the silence was at its deepest, richest, and he was good and ready, did he call off the searchlight, which returned to illuminate his grim expression.

"Elvis, stand up."

There were no family names in the Academy. Families belonged in the past for these students. Their lives were here; their lives were philosophy.

Elvis stood up.

"I take it that you find breaking wind more amusing than a trained actor slipping on a banana skin!"

Elvis cracked up. He couldn't help it.

"Enough! Have I not forbidden this? Do you not recognise the dangers? You are supposed to be a student of philosophy, not a barnyard animal with a stomach disorder."

The youth fought the urge to laugh, but without much success. When the Fat Professor was on this kind of form, it just wasn't possible to keep a straight face.

"I will not have laughter in this Hall, in this Academy, or anywhere on this planet, do you hear me? So, you leave me no choice. There is no place in this world for this outrage, not any more ... which of course means, logically, that there is no place here for *you*."

Elvis stopped laughing.

The Fat Professor smiled.

He allowed a dark silence to temporarily reign in that Great Hall, and then he broke it a final time.

"You will be taken from here to the Plato Portal and from there you will be launched into exile."

"Exile?" said Elvis. "But ... exile where?"

"There is only one place fit for the likes of you, though it appals me to even speak the word."

A thousand throats swallowed.

"You will be banished to ... *Earth*."

2. EXILE

It was decided by Walton Flowers that Elvis be taken to the Dungeon on the Hill, beneath the Plato Portal. From there, at the stroke of midnight, he would be launched into permanent exile. He would be allowed three visitors prior to dispatch, in line with the current law on exile procedure, followed by a final visit from the Fat Professor himself at thirty minutes to dispatch.

Elvis asked to see George, John and Ryan. The rules stated that they would visit separately and for not more than six minutes each. Elvis had lost count of the hours he had already spent alone in the dungeon when George arrived. But according to his friend it was already eight in the evening.

"Can you believe it?" said Elvis. "Exiled for breaking wind!"

"I thought it was for laughing," said George.

"Well, that's alright then! That makes perfect sense! I was in trouble for not laughing at his pathetic banana skin joke, and then for laughing after he'd banned laughter. But officially I'm being exiled for, wait for it ... *Crimes against Philosophy.* Can you believe that?"

"I can believe almost anything when it comes to Walton Flowers," said George, shaking his head.

Elvis grinned. "I prefer to think I'm being exiled for farting ... and on *trumped up* charges."

"You're taking it well," said George. "I thought you'd be gutted."

"I'm trying to remain philosophical," said Elvis. "And retain my sense of humour. After all, what's worth getting into a stew about? I can't do anything to change it. And anyway ..."

"You're not going to tell me that you've found a silver lining?"

Elvis began laughing. "See, they can't stop me laughing now, can they? They've already done the worst thing that they could do to me, and I'm still having a good time. And on Earth, unless things have changed in the last few hours, they're still laughing. It's the one thing that they know how to do. Here we study philosophy but there it's fun, fun, fun."

"Not according to the Professor," said George.

"What does he know? He wouldn't know fun if it bit him on his great fat arse. Take my word for it, George. On Earth it's just one big party. The place was made for teenagers. I'm going to have the time of my life – though I might have to give up philosophy in the process. And wouldn't that be a tragedy!"

Elvis was laughing again, and making George decidedly nervous.

"But you won't see any of us again. You won't see your mates, or your family, ever again."

Elvis stopped laughing. Suddenly he didn't feel the least bit like laughing.

"Mate," said George, "we're going to miss you."

Elvis shook his friend's hand and then the two of them embraced.

"You don't want to go, do you?" said George. "Not really. Is there nothing you can do? Why don't you tell Walton Flowers that you're sorry?"

"What – and that I'll never laugh or break wind again? Anyway, he's not the sort to change his mind. There's no way out so I've just got to make the best of it. What else can I do?"

George looked full; about ready to cry. "Why Earth? And where is the place, exactly?"

"It's through the Plato Portal. It doesn't exist in our world. To understand you need a history lesson and I don't think we have time for that right now."

Elvis was right. The buzzer sounded and it was time for nothing more than goodbye. The history lesson would have to wait for Ryan.

*

It was almost two hours later when Ryan was finally allowed into the dungeon for his final few minutes with his friend. He wasn't expecting a history lesson, but he got one all the same.

"Listen," said Elvis before his friend even had chance to join him on the hard stone floor. "You have to know this."

And so Elvis told him about the Time of the Great Philosophers. How the greatest philosopher of all, Plato, had discovered portals to other worlds, and had left Stone to set up academies throughout the universe.

How, according to legend, Plato's great vision had floundered when he went to Earth. And how Earth had become the graveyard for failed philosophers and the perfect place for exile ever since.

By the time Elvis had finished off the history lesson, Ryan's six minutes were almost up.

"Why are you telling me all this now?" he said. "It doesn't save you. In less than two hours they'll take you to the Plato Portal and send you to that Philosopher's Graveyard and we'll never see you again."

Elvis nodded. "Sounds pretty grim when you put it like that, doesn't it?"

"How else do you want me to put it? You'll never see your friends again. You'll have no chance of one day getting back to your family."

"There's always hope."

"Is there? Even the great Plato couldn't get back here apparently."

Elvis looked at his friend. "From what I've told you, wouldn't you say that Walton Flowers was better suited to Earth than I am?"

Ryan looked baffled by the question. But then his expression lightened. "What are you saying? You mean – there's a way to do that?"

"Spread the word," said Elvis. "When they take me to the Plato Portal, the energy they use to fire me from this world is misery, and primarily mine. But one miserable person isn't generally enough, and so they round up the most miserable people they can find and make them all chant an incantation. In this case it will be: 'Elvis – Earth.'"

"And that's all it takes?" asked Ryan.

"Simple, isn't it? But then Plato really was some genius. But Walton Flowers isn't. I won't be miserable because I have a plan and I know my history. I start laughing and Flowers gets all worked up. He becomes the miserable one – he's that already most of the time. And at just before midnight, you get all of the students to chant: 'Walton Flowers – Earth.' And that will do it."

Time was up.

Ryan was ushered out of the dungeon.

*

An hour later John walked in. When the door was safely closed behind him, leaving the two friends alone, Elvis said, "You've been talking to Ryan?"

"I certainly have. You think it will work?"

"It's practically guaranteed to. It's been done before. In the days of the revolution that we never talk about because we're forbidden to know about it. But they tried to send the revolutionaries to various parts of the universe, and many did go. Until one of them worked out how the Plato Portal worked and used it to send the counter-revolutionaries instead. They don't teach *that* at the Academy."

John smiled, but quickly his smile clouded over. "But what happens when Walton Flowers is sent in your place? What will they do to you for that?"

"Make me Professor, probably. And then the first thing I'll do is restore laughter to its rightful place at the top of the curriculum."

"Wow," said John. "And all we have to do is chant: 'Walton Flowers – Earth'?"

"That'll do it. Start at one minute to midnight and keep going until the hour is passed. Then it's goodbye Fat Professor, hello laughter."

"And nothing can go wrong?"

"What could *possibly* go wrong?"

*

Walton Flowers visited Elvis in the dungeon. The Fat Professor looked serious enough, but he wasn't fooling Elvis for a minute. He knew that inside Walton Flowers was fairly bursting with forbidden laughter.

Still, the Fat Professor had to keep up appearances. Had to play to the rules of the game that he had constructed to keep Stone the way he wanted it keeping.

"I'm sorry that it has to end this way," said Flowers. "You had a bright future here on Stone. You could have been one of the greatest philosophers of the age."

"If only I hadn't broken wind," said Elvis, with mock gravity. "Whoever heard of a philosopher breaking wind? I'll bet that Plato never heard of such a thing."

"That's enough!"

"Is it? No laughing allowed, and no breaking of wind. What kind of a life is that? I'm glad to be leaving Stone. This place has nothing left, not for me."

"I didn't come here to listen to your sarcasm, young man."

"So what did you come for? Maybe you want the truth. Well then you're in luck. You banned laughter because no-one ever laughed at your jokes. They were too busy laughing at you."

"I'm warning you, Elvis."

"Warning me? Ha – that really is a laugh. What have you left to threaten me with? Isn't exile enough? Perhaps you want to sentence me to an hour of listening to you trying to tell a joke. No, I'll take the exile, every single time."

Walton Flowers looked at his watch.

"It's a pity we have to wait until midnight," he said. "A pity that this world has to endure your arrogant foolishness a second longer. I came here sorry that this had to happen. But now I'm not sorry in the slightest."

"Oh, come on," said Elvis. "You were never sorry. I was always a threat to you. Anyone with a genuine sense of humour was always going to be a threat. But answer me one thing: did you really think anyone was going to find that banana skin pratfall funny? Do you think we're a bunch of idiots in your precious Academy? Do you think we would stay if we had any choice? That we wouldn't all rather be where we belong, with our families?"

"The Academy *is* your family – *was* your family. It's all the family a genuine philosopher needs. Truth is and should be your sole concern."

"That's a laugh! Truth? You wouldn't know truth if it came up and laughed in your face. But fat chance of that happening now. Truth wouldn't dare laugh in anybody's face, not here."

Elvis shook his head. "I'm ready when you are. Just take me to the Plato Portal and do your worst. I'm ready for a life on Earth, believe me."

*

And so it was that Elvis was taken from the dungeon to the Plato Portal. In the final minutes before midnight, the miseries of the world assembled before the hole in the rock that was the only known escape from Stone.

There were a few dozen of the miseries, wretches who appeared to have lost the use of their faces. One look into the eyes of a single one of those poor souls was enough to confirm the existence of hell.

Elvis had no doubt that there was enough misery assembled to send a demoralised soul clean out of the universe. It was just as well that on the inside he was feeling like singing a song of joy.

Yet instead of singing, he waited; waited until the countdown began.

Then he began singing.

At first Walton Flowers seemed amazed that anyone would have such nerve. But then a suspicious twinkle entered his eye.

"You're fooling no-one, Elvis. The misery has you and it will fire you from this world." And with that, the chanting began, the Fat Professor leading it. *"Elvis – Earth. Elvis – Earth."*

But Elvis merely closed his mind to the sound and instead listened to the voices in his imagination; the voices of George, Ryan and John, leading the alternative chant that was ringing out through the dormitories of the Academy. *"Walton Flowers- Earth. Walton Flowers – Earth."*

If you knew your history, there was nothing to fear; nothing in this world or any other. All it would ever take to win the day was a simple act of genius.

3. THE PLATO PORTAL AND THE BOUNCE EFFECT

The chant was reaching its climax at the Plato Portal and in the dormitories too. And Walton Flowers was smelling a rat.

Elvis was just too cool. He knew something. The miseries were chanting his name and destination and there were seconds to go to the midnight hour. Yet the look in his eyes was not of fear or defeat, but victory.

Walton Flowers started to panic. There were thirty seconds to go.

What did Elvis know?

The truth was that Elvis knew a lot. And one of the things he knew was that the miseries made no difference. That it was the mind-set of the individual that counted.

It would come down to a battle of wills between Elvis and the Fat Professor. Knowing that his friends back in the dormitories were rooting for him gave him faith, and that faith in turn revealed itself as confidence, which in turn undermined the faith of Walton Flowers.

As the seconds ticked down to zero the Fat Professor looked deep into the eyes of his rebellious student and saw the truth. That it wasn't Elvis who was destined for exile that night, but Walton Flowers himself.

As the hour struck Flowers knew that he was leaving his beloved Stone forever. But he was damned if he was going alone. In a final gesture of desperation he threw himself onto the startled Elvis, screaming, "You're coming with me!"

The Plato Portal opened and it was hungry enough to accommodate the two of them. In a second they were gone.

*

"Wow," said Elvis. "Wherever this is it's paradise."

He was standing at the water's edge, the blue of the sky and the blue of the ocean meeting on the horizon. Beneath his feet the warm yellow sand felt wonderful. There was nothing like this back where he had come from; or if there was then somebody was keeping it a secret.

He turned around to see Walton Flowers grimacing. "This is a nice mess you've got us into," said the Fat Professor.

"*I* got us into? You were the one doing the exiling. Anyway, what's wrong with it? Let's have some fun. Last one in the water's a … big fat over-stuffed misery."

Elvis launched himself into the beautiful sea and within minutes had taught himself to swim. "Come on, it's lovely in here. You could do with some exercise."

Walton Flowers snarled, watching the teenager jumping into the waves, flinching with every peal of laughter that he was powerless to prevent. From what he'd read of Earth and Plato, there was no mistaking where they'd landed up.

This was the Mediterranean; a Greek island little known to the tourists. A place for sitting cross-legged and learning about the secrets of the universe, not frolicking around in the water like some fool teenager.

At last Elvis came out of the ocean, dripping and laughing. "That was the best fun I've ever had. You have to try it. Who needs Stone? You can't ban laughter here, so loosen up and get yourself in there."

The Fat Professor glared at the youth. "Sit down," he demanded.

Elvis didn't budge. "Ah, you want to take the sunbathing option," said Elvis.

"I'll take the *beating out your brains* option if you don't sit down in five seconds!"

Elvis sat down. "Okay, I'm sitting. So make it good, Fat Man. But just remember this: we're on another planet now; you have no power over me here."

Walton Flowers waited for Elvis to shut up. Then he said, "There's a Bounce Effect."

Elvis blinked. "A what?"

"We're not stuck on this beach forever, you fool. What would be the point of that? Exiles bounce. The energy accumulated to get us here doesn't dissipate as simply as that. It has momentum. We don't come to a dead stop and retire to the beach before our time. We *bounce*."

"Excuse me," said Elvis. "I have a question."

Progress at last, thought the Fat Professor. "And what is your question?"

"My question is: what the hell are you talking about?"

Before Walton Flowers had time to remonstrate at the impertinence, the beach began to grow faint, taking the ocean and its fantastic horizon with it. The two exiles were in motion again. They landed at the Acropolis.

"Ah," said Walton Flowers. "An inspired bounce. Hallowed ground indeed. We are in Athens, Greece."

"I know," said Elvis, wishing he was still at the beach. "This is where Plato set up his original Academy." He pointed to the large structure that dominated the small hillside. "That's the Parthenon where Plato and the gang used to meet. Looks to me like it's seen better days."

"The Parthenon," said the Fat Professor, "is thousands of years old. It *has* seen better days. This miserable planet has seen better days, too. The history of philosophy here is seen as merely footnotes to the work of Plato."

Walton Flowers was settling in for what promised to be a long and tedious lecture, when the Parthenon, along with the Acropolis and the hillside on which it stood, began to fade.

"No-oo, I've only just arrived," groaned Flowers. "We need more time in this remarkable place."

But his cry went unheeded and in a moment he was standing beside a large talking mouse.

"Now we're talking," said Elvis. "Disneyland, if I'm not mistaken. You must be Mickey Mouse. I've heard a lot about you."

The following hours were filled with water rides and shows, music and dancing, fun and laughter.

Walton Flowers wasn't laughing though. What kind of planet gave such a disproportionate welcome? It confirmed everything he had expected of planet Earth: a mere handful of precious seconds at the Acropolis; hours on tedious end at a theme park.

His head was pounding. He had arrived in Hell.

Elvis, on the other hand, was thinking that those who had never experienced exile didn't know what they were missing. He wondered if they couldn't offer a period of exile to all his mates back home at the Academy; a summer break to get them through the long and torturous months of unbroken study.

This was nothing short of awesome.

Yet at last it faded, as the beach and the Acropolis had faded; as the Great Wall of China and Mount Everest faded. The Great

Barrier Reef, the Pyramids, the Hanging Gardens of Babylon, the Sahara Desert, the playgrounds of Las Vegas, the skyscrapers and rock festivals in New York … all faded, some to the relief of Elvis and many to the relief of Walton Flowers.

"Some journey this," said Elvis as a new city began to materialise. "This bouncing lark is the best thing ever. Stone needs something like it, if only at weekends."

But the Fat Professor could only say, "London."

He said it in a voice filled with trepidation. This was the place he had feared the most. If he had to come to this forsaken world, why couldn't he live out his days in the footsteps of Plato, content to limit himself to the small hillside that still conjured the memory of Ancient Greece? And in times when Earth still had something going for it, before it all turned sour.

Then he saw it. The British Museum, advertising the Elgin Marbles; stolen from the Greeks. It figured, these barbarians - no culture to call their own, stealing from the rest of their own world and not caring a fig about it either.

He was a good halfway through his soliloquy on the subject when he realised that Elvis had wandered off in the direction of a Computer Games Exhibition across the road from the museum.

"I'll catch you later," Elvis shouted back to the now speechless Fat Professor.

For the first time since their arrival into exile, the two went their separate ways. Walton Flowers to a vision of Hell, Elvis to one of Heaven. And the entrance to both, as it turned out, was free.

The Fat Professor was appalled. Culture boxed up in a building like this, given away to any Tom, Dick, or Harriet tourist who happened to be passing. People not understanding or caring a jot for a thing they were seeing. And as for those Elgin Marbles …

Across the road Elvis was having the best time ever. If you were fifteen you went free for one day only. And the games! He had never seen or even imagined anything like them. In fact you didn't have to imagine anything at all; it was all there for you, so vivid and real you could almost reach out and touch it.

He fought imaginary wars in the jungle, won a speed-boat race in the ocean, scored the winning goal in a cup-final, played in a rock band in front of hundreds of thousands of adoring fans. He had even found a game that allowed him to be a famous person in history.

For a laugh he selected Plato and spent some time at the Acropolis in Ancient Greece, telling jokes to the Academy students and organising a farting contest which was won by his finest and most famous student, Aristotle.

He could hardly wait to tell Walton Flowers about that!

As the day wore on, the two exiled travellers began to experience a curious thing. There was something in the air, distinct and at the same time elusive.

A feeling that things were about to change.

4. HEAVEN AND HELL CHANGE PLACES

The endless tour of parties did, for a while, confirm in the mind of Elvis that he had indeed arrived in Heaven. And that Heaven was a place called London.

There could be no place like it anywhere else in existence. The quality of the graphics on the computer games alone proved that much.

But as the days stretched out he began to experience something that he didn't much care for.

He had never actually experienced boredom before, not even during the worst of Walton Flowers' classes. Suppressed laughter, yes; anger and irritation, of course; but not actually boredom. Yet these days of endless fun were starting to leave in their wake a restlessness that quickly grew into something darker.

With his mind wandering from the constant focus of fun Elvis began to think about Stone. The kids here in London were great fun and cool enough, but the truth was that he was missing his mates.

At even the finest, most exclusive parties that London had to offer, he found himself distracted, wishing that his friends were there to experience all of this with him.

Would he really never see them again?

Never see Stone again?

For all that was wrong with Stone – and with any world, for that matter – the planet was his home. The place he really belonged. His mates would be missing him. Everyone at the Academy would be missing him.

He began wishing he hadn't upset the Fat Professor that day in the Great Hall. Yes, Flowers had gone too far, banning laughter from Stone. But weren't there other ways of dealing with it?

They could have had enough fun laughing in secret. What was better than secret laughter? He could have organised clandestine meetings in underground dens, laughing through the night without the Fat Professor knowing a thing about it.

The sheer delight of keeping all of that laughter inside, and then pouring it out in secret with his mates - with George, with

Ryan, with John - wouldn't that have been even better than all this?

Wouldn't that have been better than exile? Better even than parties and computer games in London, even if the graphics were as good as this?

And it wasn't just his mates, it was his family too. As long as he was in the same world, on the same planet, surely there was always the chance that he would get to see them again one day.

But what chance was there of that now?

The dark boredom and gnawing sadness grew a little each day, and soon Elvis found that there was no fun left in even the grandest computer game. And as for the parties, the other kids didn't seem so keen on his company now that he was walking around with a look of misery plastered across his face all the time.

His mates back home would have asked what was wrong. They would have cared and they would have tried to help. But to the kids here, he was just a new boy on the block; an outsider, an alien. If he wouldn't join in the laughter, they would soon find a replacement who would; a better laugh who was only too glad to be at the heart of the greatest fun-filled paradise in the universe.

While Elvis was sinking further into a state of abject misery, exactly the opposite thing was happening to Walton Flowers.

The Fat Professor had, on arrival in London, not the slightest doubt that he had located Hell. And in a fit of desperation he had decided upon the only sane course of action left to him, which was to write down his experiences into a journal. In doing this, should death ever see fit to release him from this endless state of suffering, his thoughts might at least one day be made public and his observations on the evils of laughter become the source of a revolution sometime, somewhere.

Posthumous celebrity.

It was the best that most philosophers could ever hope for, after all.

But Walton Flowers didn't have to wait for death to become a celebrity.

To keep the threat of depression at bay, the Fat Professor had been writing night and day. He finished his book, '*Why I Banned Laughter*', in next to no time, and found a publisher before the ink had dried.

To his surprise the book was an instant hit, selling faster than it could be printed.

Walton Flowers had now completed a second book, *'More on Why I Banned Laughter'*, and was working on his third, *'The Philosophy of Banning Laughter'*, when his sales hit a million, securing his status as celebrity guru and revolutionary genius.

As word spread like fire, it inevitably reached the ears of his fellow exile. The popularity of the Fat Professor's theories on banning laughter, and the implications for Earth, did nothing to ease the misery that Elvis was experiencing, and the young philosopher withdrew completely from London life.

In the weeks and months that followed Walton Flowers worked with a passion that exceeded anything he had achieved back home. He was writing by night and making endless appearances on radio and television by day. His books were piling up at the top of the best-seller charts and his public speaking engagements were consistently sold out well in advance.

And as the Fat Professor climbed steadily to his position as the most influential living philosopher on the planet, Elvis took to his bed. The young genius had become too miserable for any kind of company except his own, spending his days thinking about his friends and his family, and dreaming only of Stone. He wondered if it was possible to die from sheer misery, and spent a month focusing on that single question.

It was at that time that events were about to take another turn.

Elvis was lying in his bed, contemplating another day questioning whether misery could be fatal, and whether this would be the day that he found the answer to his all-consuming question, when he suddenly sat bolt upright.

"Eureka!" he exclaimed.

The light had come back on in Elvis' head.

5. OUTLAW ELVIS

A huge crowd gathered in Hyde Park and at midday the ceremony began. Walton Flowers took to the stage to the sound of deafening applause before introducing Greg, a trained actor specialising in physical comedy.

The Fat Professor was looking splendid in his mustard suit and matching bow-tie. He'd been living well of late, and his freshly shaved features fairly beamed out to the crowd without any need for artificial illumination.

The hour had come to put his multi-million selling theories into practice.

"As those who have read my books will know, laughter is the enemy. It disguises all that is wrong with this society and is a barrier to the possibilities of any future happiness. It simply ... must ... *go*."

He gestured for his assistant to come forward.

"And so, with the help of Greg here, we will share one final laugh together before turning out the light on this dark practice forever."

*

Elvis watched the unfolding of this all-too-familiar event on a television screen in an electrical superstore a few miles from Hyde Park.

An hour earlier he had been completing his month in bed when the light had come on in his head and he had known exactly what his true purpose and mission was to be on Earth. Yet as he watched the screen he felt the gloom-clouds drifting back and wondered if it wasn't already too late.

Walton Flowers was taking a banana from his pocket and Elvis didn't have to be a genius to work out what was going to happen next.

After polishing off the fruit, the banana skin was flung down onto the stage, waiting ominously for Greg to 'just happen by', whistling a cockney tune as he approached the discarded skin.

The fall, Elvis had to admit, was impressive, and the laughter that followed entirely genuine. The entire crowd was laughing.

And they went on laughing, until Walton Flowers' face turned from sunshine to thunder, ushering in an immediate silence.

The silence was so loud that it echoed.

Elvis turned up the volume control on the television, to make certain that the sound was still working. It was working fine. And when the silence was finally broken by the sudden and rude voice of the Fat Professor, the speaker on the television set almost ruptured.

"Laughter is now forbidden. A new age has dawned here today in this City of London, and in this country that we know as Great Britain. But we must not be content to let our vision rest here within these shores alone. Our next objective is Europe, our ultimate objective ... *the world*."

*

At that point Elvis came close, perilously close, to letting the light go out entirely. The Fat Professor was on the march and nothing surely could stop him.

Only an hour ago his brain had burned with the brightness of a thousand suns, and he had known precisely what he had to do. If Walton Flowers was bent on educating the world about the evils of laughter, then his mission was to ensure that laughter never died on this planet. His mission was to show the world that laughter alone could save the world, not destroy it, as Flowers was suggesting in his pathetic books.

But already it was too late. The Fat Professor had grown too strong, had gained too deep a foothold on the planet. Had accomplished the first part in his master plan to take over the world and turn it into a dry, humourless place that would live out his rules to the letter.

And yet the light did not entirely go out in Elvis' head that day.

As he stood watching the screen in the electrical superstore, which he had been passing on his way to the British Library, he heard a voice behind him.

"Would sir be interested in purchasing that particular television?"

Elvis turned to see a thin-faced man looking at him from behind a thick pair of glasses.

"Did you see that broadcast?" asked Elvis.

"I don't believe I did, sir."

"How do you know when an elephant's been in your fridge?"

"I beg your pardon, sir?"

"Footprints in the butter."

"Sir?"

"It's a joke. You can tell an elephant's been in your fridge when you see its footprints in the butter."

"Oh, I see, sir. That is very good indeed, sir."

Then the salesman began to laugh. It was the worst imitation of laughter that Elvis had ever witnessed in his life. Thin faced weasel laughter. But it was still laughter of a kind and a spit in the eye for the Fat Professor.

A cough startled the salesman, who instantly dropped the false laughter and attempted to restore a more serious expression.

A large supervisor approached. "Mr. Bentley, did you not hear the word from Hyde Park?"

"Word, Mrs Jester?"

"Laughter is banned in this superstore and in the rest of London and Great Britain. You will refrain instantly or I shall have to call the police. Now, is that young person intending to purchase that television or not?"

Elvis left the store and decided to abandon his plan to visit the British Library. The matter had become too urgent and the luxury of research no longer an option.

He headed for the underground.

*

Walton Flowers went from strength to strength, preaching his anti-laughter doctrine throughout Europe. And once Europe was converted he moved on to the Americas, Asia and Africa. Australia was a tussle at first for the Fat Professor; the people seemed strangely reluctant to give up the gift of laughter. He wore them down though, eventually, and soon the entire planet was converted to his miserable philosophy.

And so Earth became a dry and humourless world while Walton Flowers laughed all the way to the bank. The great Philosopher-King ruled his new world and there was not a thing anybody could do about it.

There were things, however, that the Fat Professor knew nothing about, at least not yet.

Secret things.

Like underground meetings.

People, mostly teenagers, were assembling in secret places beneath the city.

Laughter dens.

The laughter dens started in the sewers but were spreading quickly, surfacing in private rooms.

One person alone was responsible for the onset of this rebellion. A philosopher with a raging, defiant belief that laughter was not only the most precious gift in the world, but that without it the world was truly doomed. He was an alien, an exile, and his name was Elvis; and he made no bones about where he had come from and why he was here.

In an early meeting, down in the sewers beneath the King's Road, he had assembled some youths who had become bored with London life, and he told them about the importance of laughter.

One of the youths, all pimples and violent habits, had suggested they get some fun out of the evening by ripping fingers out of sockets to find out how loud Elvis could scream.

Realising that the *philosophy of laughter* was wasted on the youths, Elvis instead tried out some of his finest jokes. Jokes tried and tested in the Stone Academy. Sure-fire winners that no youngster worth the name could fail to crack up at.

But no-one laughed.

"Come on," said Elvis. "No-one can hear you down here. Don't be afraid to let that laughter out. It will do you no good fighting it."

The word 'fighting' had seemed to be a cue, and the leader of the Pimple Necks edged towards Elvis menacingly. "We're not laughing because you aren't funny, mate. And down here you don't need to worry about people hearing you laughing: down here they can't hear you *scream*. Who are you, anyway?"

As they edged towards him, Elvis gave up the jokes and came clean.

"Actually, I'm a member of the Academy."

"The what?"

He explained. "A school of philosophers in a world known as Stone."

"Is he taking the Mickey? Where's this Stone, then?"

"It's a planet in another world to yours. I came here through the Plato Portal."

"He is taking the Mick. I think we've heard enough, hey, lads?"

The gang fell in behind their leader. "So tell us about this Stone? Is it run by your Fairy Godmother?"

"No, actually Stone is run by the Fat Professor."

Then it happened; that unmistakable sound. One of the youths laughed. The leader turned around, and now there was a chorus of laughter. Elvis was stunned. "No," he said, "don't stop. Let it out."

But the laughter had stopped and the leader of the Pimple Necks squared up to Elvis. "Fat Professor? Are you having a laugh?"

"The Fat Professor, also known as Walton Flowers …" said Elvis. "He sent me into exile for breaking wind in the Great Hall."

The youths halted their advance on Elvis, looked at each other, and cracked up. Their leader was down on the ground, holding his stomach, and bellowing for all he was worth.

However long they had gone without a laugh was nobody's business; it was like a drought ending. They couldn't stop. The Pimple Necks had tears running down their faces and they were begging for mercy. Elvis capitalised, firing out a string of anecdotes about the Fat Professor and his infamously bad jokes.

By the time he'd finished, their stomachs were aching and their throats raw. They thought it was the best time they'd had in years and insisted that they meet again the following night, when they could bring more of their mates down.

Elvis' reputation spread until London could no longer contain him. And once the secret was out it was only a matter of time before word reached the ears of Walton Flowers, back from a lecture tour of the Maldives, where he had also been researching a book on how not to laugh whilst touring paradise on a private yacht the size of a small town.

"*Elvis*," he muttered to himself, on hearing the news. "*That thorn in my backside!*"

An urgent appearance by Walton Flowers on national television climaxed with the words: "There is amongst us a plague that will destroy not merely London, not merely Britain; a plague that will not stop at Europe, that knows, that recognises, no borders in land, sea or sky; a plague that will consume this entire planet, a plague that has one name … *Elvis*."

The Fat Professor's face filled the camera along with a nation's television screens as it pronounced sentence: "No …" he almost said *stone* … "rock will be left unturned until we have this outlaw behind bars. It is the priority of this great nation, and indeed the priority of the world, that he is caught, and caught *today*."

*

In the days following the broadcast, Elvis would show the clip in laughter dens throughout the British Isles, usually at the beginning or end of a meeting. It never failed to get the biggest laugh and was regularly demanded as an encore.

Everywhere Elvis travelled, under the cover of darkness and always in disguise, he was met with the medicine of laughter. They were the best times. At the end of a particularly raucous meeting in a sound-proofed basement in Glasgow, he told the assembled laughers of his plans.

"Tonight we are laughing here in Scotland and tomorrow we will be laughing … where?"

He eyed the crowded room. The laughers here were all ages, from all backgrounds. "Timbuktu!" shouted an old college professor in a well-worn tweed suit. "Aunty Margaret's!" shouted a young boy, earning a pat on the head from his proud father. "Atlantis!" shouted a young hairdresser with a wooden leg, trying to be clever but nevertheless getting a generous laugh for her troubles.

"All those places," said Elvis from the make-shift stage. "But first we take Europe. We bring the gift of laughter back to the French, the Germans, the Dutch, and the Spanish. Have I missed anybody out?"

The crowd shouted out the names of every country in Europe.

"Yes indeed. We will bring them all back together with the gift more precious than gold or immortality. We will laugh Europe back together and then we will do the same for the world."

The applause was the finest Elvis had ever heard. And he smiled.

*

The Laughter Wars, as they became known, raged across Europe for months before spreading throughout the entirety of inhabited Earth. Walton Flowers' crusade to wipe out laughter from the world was nothing less than vicious, while Elvis fought with an equal passion, untiring and inspired, to ensure that wherever human beings walked the planet laughter went with them, whether in public or in private.

On the Fat Professor's orders, the prisons of the world were emptied of thieves and murderers, and filled instead with those who dared to laugh out loud. It was estimated that, should Elvis ever be caught, he would face a jail term in excess of a billion years for his laughter crimes.

"I'd better start working on the Philosopher's Stone after all," was his response on hearing the estimate. "Get myself some immortality so I don't die before I've served my sentence."

Elvis travelled the globe in his efforts to spread his message and urge resistance throughout all the lands. His words about the Philosopher's Stone were spoken to an underground reporter and then 'leaked' to all the major newspapers and television networks world-wide. The sad consequence, however, was that more than a thousand people, on hearing or reading this, laughed publicly and found themselves in prison for their sins.

For every such outrage, Elvis worked harder, spreading his belief that, despite the risks, laughter was too precious to be allowed to be eradicated. "Laughter is no longer a laughing matter. It has become serious. It has become the most serious issue facing your world today. Laughter is a gift – the most precious gift in this world or any other. Without it ... civilisation cannot exist."

Those words, spoken by Elvis at a mass underground laughing event in Northern California, circled the globe in hours, thanks to a hungry global media desperate for anything connected to the hottest potato of the day.

But those words proved to be far more historic than Elvis could ever have predicted, even with his planet-sized brain. Historic because they were the final words he would publicly utter as an outlaw from the 'justice' demanded by Walton Flowers.

One day later, spreading his message in the labyrinthine laughter dens of Mexico, a note was handed to him by a mysterious stranger.

The stranger had entered the den during a screening of one of the Fat Professor's London lectures. As far as Elvis was concerned, the deadly-serious lectures of Walton Flowers were the funniest things in existence. Masterpieces of unintentional humour, and they never failed with any crowd, regardless of age, race, gender or religion. The sheer pomposity, unbearable under normal circumstances, could reduce a legion of grim-faced bureaucrats to gibbering wrecks in under a minute. Lawyers, teachers, even politicians – no-one was immune.

Once you saw the funny side of the Fat Professor, it would take a team of surgeons with very sharp knives indeed to get the smile off your face.

The crowd of converts had been laughing themselves crazy when Elvis noticed the stranger out of the corner of his eye. Apart from the wide-brimmed hat and gunfighter charisma, the stranger stood out from the crowd due to the fact that he didn't so much as crack a smile.

Intrigued, Elvis approached him, and was handed the curious message.

"I need to speak to you in private," said the stranger.

In a small room, with the sounds of laughter pummelling the walls as the crowd continued to appreciate the unintentional wit of the Fat Professor, Elvis opened the envelope that the stranger had handed to him.

What he read took his breath away.

He looked at the stranger. "This is impossible," he said.

6. SIGNALS FROM A DYING WORLD

At first Elvis thought it was some kind of joke, and one in the worst possible taste.

But there was only one other person who had the knowledge to make such a joke: Walton Flowers himself.

Elvis looked again at the note. To anybody else reading it, all they would see was incomprehensible squiggles. But out of those squiggles arose a name more terrifying than any other.

Theodore Dee.

It was a name that, unlike the name 'Walton Flowers', failed to raise even a smile.

There was nothing good in the name 'Theodore Dee'. No saving grace. No hidden silver lining. It was a dark cloud with an even darker lining.

"Where did you get this?" asked Elvis.

One of the few scientists left south of the border with any sense of humour had been experimenting with the notion of portals to and from other worlds. Down among the ancient catacombs cut into a hillside in the north of the country, he had found traces of distant signals and attempted to respond to them. It had been slow and laborious work, and none of the received signals acknowledged receipt of any sent ones.

But still the signals kept coming.

"The Plato Portal," said Elvis, but the stranger merely frowned.

"This is the work of George, Ryan and John."

Again the stranger registered nothing more than bafflement.

"Stone is dying."

"Stone?"

"Theodore Dee has taken over my world and Stone is dying under his brutal regime."

The stranger said, "I haven't a clue what you're talking about. I was told to be bring you this note."

"Yes," said Elvis. "And thank you. You couldn't possibly know about Stone or about Theodore Dee. Let's just say that he's like Walton Flowers but without the sense of humour."

"That sounds bad."

"Bad is one word you could use. But it would hardly be sufficient."

"Who is this Theodore Dee?"

"He's a Fat Professor."

"You get a lot of Fat Professors on Stone?"

"Far too many, though none fatter or more professorial than Theodore Dee believe me."

"What are you going to do about it?"

"There is only one thing I can do," said Elvis.

"What's that?"

"Get back to Stone."

"And how are you going to do that?"

Elvis shrugged. "It's never been done. I haven't the first clue. But I know someone who might."

"Who would that be?"

Elvis smiled. "If I told you … you would only laugh."

*

Elvis booked himself on a flight to London. On arrival he took a cab from Heathrow airport to an exclusive apartment in Mayfair. He was heavily disguised as a Chinese business man, and the cab-driver kept giving him strange looks through the rear-view mirror.

At the apartment block security was tight; and when Elvis asked to see the Fat Professor he was asked for his details.

Elvis wrote his name on a card and placed it into a sealed envelope.

"Give this to Walton Flowers and he will see me."

Within the minute Elvis was searched before being escorted along a rich, velvet-lined corridor, towards the entrance to the most exclusive apartment in the whole of London.

The entrance hall was decorated with solid gold and encrusted with diamonds, while white tigers padded over the deep red carpet and men with machine-guns and miserable faces stood like statues around the doorway to the apartment.

The door opened and Elvis went inside.

*

The place was like a palace and the interior entrance hall appeared to stretch for miles. Six armed guards escorted Elvis along the winding trail until they came to a smaller doorway leading to a candle-lit room. Here

Elvis was searched a second time before being ushered into the room.

Behind him the door closed and for a few moments Elvis stood in the candle-lit silence. Then, from a remote corner of the room, a familiar figure stepped into view.

"Giving yourself up then, are we?"

Elvis nodded. "Something like that."

"Well, I think you can dispense with the ridiculous fancy dress now at least. Is that any way for a Stone Philosopher to be seen about town?"

"Theodore Dee," said Elvis.

"What did you say?"

"You heard me."

"That name - what about him?"

"He's taken over."

Walton Flowers didn't so much sit down as collapse dramatically into one of his over-stuffed armchairs.

After taking a full minute to regain some composure he eyed Elvis suspiciously. "How could you possibly know this?"

Elvis tried to explain what he had heard about the Mexican scientist conducting experiments on portals and discovering signals from the Plato Portal.

After he had given his explanation, the room again fell silent. Then something utterly amazing happening.

The Fat Professor began laughing. It wasn't just a titter or a chuckle, either, but a full-blown belly laugh.

When he had finished Elvis said, "Not practising what you preach then I see?"

"Are you accusing me of hypocrisy, young Elvis?"

"If the cap fits then wear it."

"Oh, how very droll: you evidently have not been studying your political philosophy. If you had you would know that when it comes to power, those who make the rules cannot be bound by them. That would make no sense at all."

"You think that's fair?"

"Fair? What's *fair* to do with anything? It's the way things work, in this world and any other. Besides, I have an elevated sense of humour. I can hardly be expected not to laugh at my own jokes – for who could resist them? It is the price one pays for being a comic genius of the first order."

"You've never made me laugh," said Elvis. "Except when you're trying to be serious – then you're unstoppable."

The smile vanished from the Fat Professor's face in an instant, and he cleared his throat. "So," he said, "back to this nonsense about messages from Stone."

"It isn't nonsense."

"What proof have you? How do I know this isn't some plot you're hatching?"

"Stone is dying," said Elvis. "We have to find a way back home to save our world before it's too late."

"Ah, now I see," said Flowers. "The great genius doesn't know how to get home. The great genius thinks I'm going to arrange to have him flown out of exile and back to Stone. That's why you're here, isn't it? Do you imagine that all I have to do is book you a seat and wish you *bon voyage*! Do you imagine I would do that even if I could? You've got a nerve, Elvis, coming here with your cock and bull tale and expecting me to help you, you really have."

"This isn't a game," said Elvis. "Stone is really dying."

"Proof, Elvis. Proof or be damned!"

*

Elvis was allowed to make some phone calls, and the following day the Mexican scientist duly arrived at the Mayfair apartment. The Fat

Professor listened carefully to everything the scientist had to say, and then startled the poor man by laughing in his face.

"I didn't realise that laughing was allowed," said the scientist, somewhat perplexed.

"Ha!" said Flowers. "That was ironic laughter. There is a distinction. I can't expect a mere man of science to understand that distinction, naturally. Anyway, what you have told me hardly constitutes proof that you have actually received messages from Stone. Frankly, you are wasting my time. Good day to you."

The scientist was taken away and the Fat Professor eyeballed Elvis.

"Any more bright ideas?"

Elvis thought for a moment. Then he said, "Why not take a trip to Mexico?"

"I've wasted enough time on this tomfoolery."

"Look," said Elvis, "if there's any chance at all that the Plato Portal is active from Earth, why not explore it? We could get home."

Walton Flowers looked at him but didn't say anything.

"Perhaps you don't want to get home," said Elvis. "Perhaps you're having too much fun here. Maybe you're afraid of Theodore Dee."

The Fat Professor's face turned purple almost instantly. When he spoke, the rage bubbled on his breath dangerously, though his voice remained creepily quiet.

"Do you not think, Elvis, that I have done everything in my power to find the Plato Portal from here? I returned to the beach on which we first arrived in this world. I found the very spot where we first entered exile and I found nothing. Stone is my home. I belong there. If there was a way back I would take it."

"Would you?" said Elvis. "Would you give up power and glory here to play second fiddle to Theodore Dee?"

The Fat Professor's voice exploded. "I play second fiddle to nobody, here or there." Then he picked up the nearest phone. "Get me a flight to Mexico. Now!"

*

The two exiles from Stone followed the scientist down and down again, mile on mile, into the ancient catacombs hidden deep inside the Mexican hillside. It was like entering villages of the dead.

All the while Walton Flowers was chuntering on about this being a great waste of his valuable time. But Elvis knew that he was making noises to escape the dreadful, chilling silence of the place.

After what seemed like an endless confusion of passages lined with the dead, they entered a small chamber. It was scarcely large enough to contain the three of them, as Walton Flowers had gained some considerable weight during his time on Earth.

They squeezed around a tiny opening in a hidden corner of the chamber. The opening was about the size of an average thumb but most definitely smaller than one of the Fat Professor's thumbs.

This small opening, according to the scientist, was the source of the signals.

In an adjacent, larger chamber, the scientist had set up an impressive array of equipment, and he explained the various items of apparatus to Elvis and to the rather impatient Flowers.

The recorded sounds, according to the scientist, were nothing more than seemingly random beeps, and the captured light transmissions apparently nothing more than random flashes. Yet the highly sensitive equipment was programmed to establish patterns according to every known system of what the scientist referred to as "logic and code". In this way words such as STONE; DYING; THEODORE and DEE had been established along with the words ELVIS and HELP.

"Logic!" said Walton Flowers, once the scientist had finished. "What does this world know of logic? Give me that equipment. I'll get to the bottom of this."

*

Elvis had to admit that even he was impressed. As for the scientist, he was nothing short of bewildered at the Fat Professor's astonishing display of logical and scientific brilliance as he grappled with the incoming codes.

After a couple of hours Walton Flowers took a break from his labours.

"Might I say, that was rather impressive," said the scientist.

"Nonsense," said the Fat Professor. "Science is a cinch. It's philosophy you want to catch up on. Now, I would conclude that the signals appear to be from Stone, on the face of it." At this point he looked at Elvis. "However, I have been unable to verify beyond doubt that the signals were indeed generated from our planet. They could have been transmitted from virtually anywhere, including Earth."

Elvis shook his head. "You still don't trust me, do you? You think I'm plotting something."

Flowers' eyes narrowed. "And are you?"

"I just want to get home," said Elvis. "They need us, both of us."

Walton Flowers returned to his labours, bewildering the scientist further by sending a series of cryptic, apparently nonsensical messages to a series of obscure co-ordinates derived from impossibly complex equations that he insisted on doodling onto a notepad.

Then the breakthrough came.

A response to one of his messages encrypted with clear Stone logic. Elvis looked at it and confirmed what the Fat Professor already suspected: that the response was directly from the Academy.

And, thought Elvis, more specifically, from George, Ryan and John.

With a sudden gush of generosity Walton Flowers said, "Your friends do credit to the Academy. They were obviously taught well. In fact I would say that they were taught by nobody less than the finest philosopher in existence – there, here, or anywhere else."

He then spent the next five minutes waxing lyrical about the virtues of home, only to be cut short by Elvis. "It's a pity, as you love Stone so much, that you've been wasting so much time making money out of misery here."

Flowers was about to respond, but got only so far as to open his mouth, before closing it again. In the strange silence that resonated around the chamber, Elvis wondered if he didn't hear the sound of a penny dropping; or whether *that* was merely wishful thinking.

Using the codes and co-ordinates constructed by Flowers, Elvis sent a series of messages asking for more information on the construction of the portal and evidence of past transportation. But the signal seemed weaker and Elvis was having difficulty translating the information into any intelligible form.

"If you want a job doing – do it yourself," muttered the Fat Professor, with an air of desperation. Then, pushing Elvis out of the way, he took over the controls once again and sent a few messages of his own.

But the returning signal was every bit as weak now as it had been when Elvis tried, and becoming weaker with every attempt.

"I think," said the scientist, "that the portal is closing down."

"I think," said Flowers, "that you have spoken sense for the first time in a long time. I think you are right. The portal is indeed closing down."

7. THE MIDDLE WAY OR THE PHILOSOPHY OF LAUGHTER

The career of Walton Flowers now took two separate paths. In private he filled up endless pages with furious, passionate outpourings, bucking against a dictator more extreme even than himself. Theodore Dee: a vicious tyrant ruling Stone with an iron fist, bringing the beloved homeland to its knees.

Theodore Dee, he wrote, *is killing my world and there's not a thing I can do about it save fill up these pages like a schoolboy writing out lines that nobody will ever read.*

But publicly the Fat Professor was writing a very different book: '*A Definitive Philosophy of Laughter.*' According to the new philosophy that Walton Flowers was now keen to try out on Earth, there was a *Middle Way*.

It seemed, in the world according to Walton Flowers, that it was now possible to combine responsibility with fun; laughter with philosophy.

In the face of initial hostility towards these radical new ideas, the Fat Professor vehemently denied accusations that he was staging a complete turnaround from his earlier philosophy. He maintained that it was all part of an inevitable and entirely historic process. Earth first had to give up laughter before it could appreciate its value and its proper place. The time was now right for the new phase: for the *Middle Way*.

And the world bought this new philosophy hook, line and sinker. Sales were even greater than for his previous best-sellers, and even the term 'publishing phenomenon' didn't do justice to what Walton Flowers was achieving.

He had to confess – in private, naturally – that perhaps he had been a little harsh in his initial valuation of Earth. Perhaps the place had been unfairly represented in Stone's literature after all.

Yet despite his unprecedented success with '*A Definitive Philosophy of Laughter*', the Fat Professor could find no rest from the relentless anxiety he was feeling for his beloved Stone. Regardless of his astonishing sales figures and status as Philosopher King of Planet Earth, he remained powerless to stop

Theodore Dee from carrying through the atrocities that would eventually, if unchecked, bring about the final destruction of his own world.

*

Elvis, meanwhile, was hunting frantically, high and low, for another site of the elusive Plato Portal. He had returned to the beach in Greece, hunted through the sewers of London, revisited the locations where the laughter dens had been the most triumphant, as well as the places where Walton Flowers had found his greatest successes. Scientists were measuring signal activity in every corner of the globe, and all, so far, to no avail.

And then it came: as Elvis returned to visit Flowers in that palatial apartment in Mayfair, London: *the moment of discovery.*

"It wasn't just underneath your nose all the time," said Elvis. "But under your big fat backside!"

"I must ask you to watch your language, young man," retorted Flowers. "That is no way to speak to a Professor."

It turned out that the new portal, many times more powerful than the one found amongst the catacombs of the ancient dead deep within a Mexican hillside, was located in the toilet bowl situated in the Fat Professor's most private quarters.

"You place your bottom over that portal every single morning, without the slightest idea of what kind of signals you're sending."

"Do you mind!" said Walton Flowers. "My toilet habits are my own business, and I would prefer it that such information remains strictly confidential. Do you understand?"

Elvis understood alright.

"Anyway, what were you doing using my own private facilities, and why have you invited that Mexican scientist here? Don't you think we can manage perfectly well without him? Scientists on this planet, Mexican or otherwise, need to brush up on their philosophy, like I said before, instead of messing with the dafter end of science."

Elvis answered in reverse order.

"In answer to your second question: I invited the Mexican because he would seem to be the most likely person to get us out of here. And 'daft', is it, utilising science to aid our returning to our homeland before Theodore Dee destroys it?"

"You know perfectly well what I mean," said Flowers.

Elvis didn't, but he let the matter go and instead answered the first question.

"As for why I was using the 'royal toilet bowl', let's just say that I happened to be passing and that I was desperate at the time. This rich diet you insist on here is doing me no good at all."

"Sort out your own food arrangements, if that's your attitude," said Flowers. "It's a wretch who bites the hand that feeds him."

"Which philosopher said that? No, let me guess. But more to the point, you never said that the toilet in there was for your arse only."

"I've warned you before about language. Try to conduct yourself in a manner becoming of a so-called philosophical genius."

"On one condition," said Elvis.

"What condition?"

"The scientist stays."

*

The equipment was set up and the Mexican scientist became only the third person permitted to enter the private facilities belonging to Walton Flowers. The Fat Professor quickly established contact with Stone, the signals coming through strongly and coherently. Still the scientist remained sceptical at the speed at which the complex coding systems were translated into comprehensible dialogue.

"You have much to learn on this little world," the Fat Professor told him, and using his best patronising tone. "And should your kind ever learn the skills required to use this portal for your own adventures, well, Stone always welcomes visitors who come in peace. Isn't that right, Elvis?"

But Elvis was distracted by the latest message returning from Stone.

Walton Flowers, oblivious to this, was still spouting on about Stone's hospitality and generosity.

"... If we can share a little of our profound wisdom with the less fortunate worlds – like your own, for example – then it brings a warm glow to a Stone heart. It's like this situation that we have here. I could close my bathroom door and conduct all of this in private – yet I choose to let you observe. That is true openness, Stone through and through, isn't that right, Elvis?"

When Elvis again didn't respond, the Fat Professor turned to see his young student checking through the data spilling out of the toilet bowl.

"... You see, this is really a very straightforward matter indeed – at least, it is for a Stone Philosophy Professor. We simply ask for the co-ordinates that will enable us to return to our world. Not exactly ... *rocket science*, is it?"

Walton Flowers filled the room with laughter, shaking his head as though at a loss as to how he could be so consistently amusing.

Once his own laughter had died down he attempted to sum up Stone for the benefit of the scientist. "Peace," he said. "Generosity," he added. "Openness," he continued. "Not forgetting," he said, as though he had forgotten and was desperately scrambling to remember. "Sharing," he blurted out. "Tolerance," he declared, almost triumphantly, as though completing a challenging assignment in memory recall. "And, of course, we lead the way when it comes to philosophical ..."

Elvis coughed until he had Flowers' attention.

"What is it?" snapped the Fat Professor.

"I think you should see this," said Elvis.

"Read it out, can't you? Do you have the co-ordinates?"

"That's the problem. They won't communicate with you."

"What?"

"The co-ordinates can only be given … to me."

"Give me that!"

Flowers snatched the data from Elvis and, purpling with rage and with the stated Stone virtues of peace, generosity, openness, sharing and tolerance appearing to be long forgotten already, he responded by sending back a message of his own.

"Wait till they read that! I'll wake them up and bring them back to their senses. I never heard of such a thing."

The message came back fast and clear.

"Read it out then. Let's see how they've changed their tune."

Elvis hesitated.

"Come on, what's the matter with you?" thundered the Fat Professor.

Elvis read the message from Stone. "Walton Flowers isn't welcome here. We already have one dictator in the shape of Theodore Dee. We will give the co-ordinates to you and you alone. Come back. We need you."

Walton Flowers was speechless.

Elvis broke the wretched silence. "Leave it to me," he said.

"What, so that you can escape back to Stone and leave me here?"

"I wouldn't do that. If we are to defeat Theodore Dee – and it pains me to have to say it, but, here goes: *Stone needs you*. There, I've said it."

"Oh, so you would include me in your plans because I'm of some use to you, is that it?"

"You want blood," said Elvis. "Look, they remember you as you were: as a dictator. They don't trust you. But you can show them you've changed; and you can earn back their trust."

"Earn? You think I owe them anything?"

Walton Flowers stopped in his tracks, and his voice softened almost to a whisper.

"Me – a *dictator*?"

"What was the last thing you did before you left Stone?"

"You mean …?"

"Exactly," said Elvis. "You banished laughter. How are they supposed to remember you?"

The Fat Professor sat down on his toilet seat. "I see."

Walton Flowers looked a sad and lonely man as he sat there on his golden throne, his face cupped in his hands, his long sighs as deep as the rivers of misery that ran through the universe.

Elvis looked at the scientist, who was clearly a man of some emotion. There was something resembling a tear in the scientist's eye, though he quickly turned away and pretended to be retrieving a rogue eyelash or some other foreign object.

Turning back to the lost and forlorn Walton Flowers, Elvis said, "Listen, this is what I'm going to do."

But the Fat Professor wasn't listening. He was too busy forming his own sad soliloquy. "I've been a fool, young Elvis. And now not only must I suffer, consigned to remain in exile all of my days, but Stone must suffer too, dying under the brutal hand of Theodore Dee."

Elvis could take not another second of this outrageous self-pity, and he shouted, "Shut up and listen, will you, for once in your life?"

Walton Flowers looked at Elvis, his mouth gaping open, his self-pitying soliloquy abandoned. Even the scientist had stopped messing with his eye.

"As I was saying," said Elvis.

Flowers and the scientist listened.

"I intend telling them how you've changed; that you're not the man who left Stone, no longer the man who banned laughter. They will only give the co-ordinates to me because they don't trust you. They expect that you'd use them for your own ends and leave me here in exile. I can convince them but I have to deal with them alone and you have to trust me."

Walton Flowers looked at the young philosopher.

"You do credit to the Academy, Elvis. I'm proud of you. There is hope for Stone with a generation like you around. Do what you have to do. And if there's anything I can do to assist, just give the word."

"Well," said Elvis, "you can start by shifting your backside off that seat. I need to use your toilet again and urgently."

*

Alone in the bathroom Elvis sent a message to Stone. George, Ryan and John in turn responded. They didn't trust the Fat Professor, not for a second. But at the same time they accepted that defeating Theodore Dee without him was an impossibility. Dee was ripping their world apart and if they didn't return to Stone soon it would be too late.

They sent the co-ordinates.

*

With Walton Flowers allowed back in his precious bathroom, and a poignant and heartfelt thank you given to the Mexican scientist, who again seemed to have something in his eye, Elvis punched in the numbers on the apparatus and prepared to depart Earth for Stone.

The two philosophers issued a chorus of farewells and waved at the scientist, who was still rubbing at his face. But the scientist did not appear to be getting any fainter.

"Why are you still here, man?" said the Fat Philosopher.

Elvis checked the apparatus and punched the numbers in a second time. Another chorus of goodbyes followed, yet still the scientist could clearly be seen rubbing at his eye.

"We don't appear to be getting anywhere," said Walton Flowers at last, clearly not having lost his talent for stating the obvious.

"Third time lucky?" suggested Elvis, punching in the numbers a final time.

"I'm not given to superstition," retorted Flowers.

Another chorus of goodbyes followed and then the scientist, as visible as ever, finally stopped messing with his troublesome eye. The Stone Philosophers were clearly going nowhere.

8. JUST ANOTHER STROKE OF GENIUS

"There's an energy issue," said Elvis. "We need to generate more of it."

"How much energy *can* you generate in a modest bathroom?" asked the Fat Professor.

The scientist tried to contribute, suggesting, amongst other things, the use of nuclear fission.

"We want transporting back to Stone, not blowing to smithereens!" said Flowers.

Elvis attempted to calm the situation. "Look, I think we need to give this some thought. It's not going to help if we all get frustrated and start shouting at each other. I say we take a break and get our heads together."

*

But the break did no good at all, and quickly the frustrations grew.

"The solution's simple," said Elvis, the three of them back in the bathroom, struggling to combine their wisdom.

The other two were looking at him, expectantly.

"... If we could only see it ..."

"Idiot!" thundered Flowers. "I thought you had it!"

"Well, I haven't heard anything constructive from you for a while, as it happens."

The scientist tried to intervene, and for his trouble received a blistering tirade from the Fat Professor.

"I don't know why you're even here! Is there nothing you could be getting on with back in Mexico? It's all take, take, take with you Earthlings. We teach you our philosophies, invite you into our bathrooms, and when it comes to the tiny matter of blasting us back through the Plato Portal situated in *my* toilet bowl, what do you contribute? Tell me that, man?"

Then Flowers started to laugh.

"Hey, listen to this: how many scientists does it take to send a Fat Professor and his 'genius' student through the Plato Portal in his golden toilet, out of Exile on Earth, and back to Stone to fight oppression in the shape of Theodore Dee?"

Elvis and the scientist looked at each other and sighed.

"Okay," said Flowers, "here's another one. And this one's even better, in my opinion. How many philosophers does it take …?"

The Fat Professor had to sit back on his gold toilet seat, weak with laughing so hard at his own lame attempts at humour.

Elvis was losing the will to live. "You know something?" he said. "I liked you better miserable. At least you were funny then."

Walton Flowers considered the observation for a moment, and then exploded with even louder laughter. When he finally stopped, a serious expression took over his fat face. "You, Elvis, are truly a genius. You have given me the greatest idea of this age. It's simple."

"The best ideas usually are," said Elvis.

"The paradox of laughter itself," said Flowers, shaking with excitement. "We are stuck here, exiled forever, but every cloud has indeed a silver lining. I intend to produce nothing less than a thirteen part treatise expounding my Philosophy of Laughter. I will go further than I or anybody else has gone before on the subject, and it will be the last word."

"Why thirteen parts?" asked the scientist, nervously.

"Why not?" said Flowers. "It seems just the right length to me. But what would an Earth scientist know of such matters?"

He turned to Elvis. "What do you think of my little project?"

"Do you want the truth?"

"I demand nothing less than the truth, at all times and in all places."

"I think," said Elvis, "that it could spell the end of laughter forever."

The Fat Professor's face dropped. "Does the truth have to always be so brutal with you?"

"I'm afraid," said Elvis, "in this case it does. Laughter doesn't need text books explaining it. All that can do is destroy it, and it's far too precious for that. At least when you were banning it there were rebels who would buck against such stupidity and keep the gift alive. You didn't know it but you were laughter's best friend; you were its saviour. But a thirteen part treatise on the subject – that really could kill it for good. Even I couldn't fight that kind of stupidity."

"You've made your point."

Then the Fat Professor noticed something. A strange expression had formed on the face of the young philosopher.

"Elvis … *what is it?*"

"Laughter," said Elvis.

"What about it?"

"The energy we need."

"You're not making any sense."

"Listen," said Elvis. "We've overlooked the obvious. I knew the solution would be simple – the best ones always are. And believe me, this is one of the very best."

"What on *Earth* are you talking about?" asked Walton Flowers.

"Don't you see?" said Elvis, his eyes glowing with excitement. "We need laughter, buckets of the stuff, and we have to focus it here, in your bathroom, in your toilet bowl. Enough of the stuff – the genuine stuff – will generate the energy we need to get us back to Stone."

*

For the best part of three hours they told each other the finest jokes they knew. But under the pressure of trying to laugh, even some of Elvis' favourites didn't seem the least bit funny anymore. It was hopeless; the more they tried to force the laughter, the less they felt like laughing and the less funny everything seemed.

The scientist tried to break the gloom by sending out word that the world's funniest jokes were required, urgently. Elvis demanded the same from Stone.

The finest comedians on Earth sent their best jokes to the Mexican scientist, while Elvis set his mates at the Academy the task of rounding up the finest humour that Stone had to offer.

But no matter how inspired the jokes seemed to one of them, another wouldn't get it at all. What made the scientist laugh rarely caused as much as a chuckle from Elvis. And Walton Flowers appeared to operate on a different level of humour from the other two entirely.

The Fat Professor was back on his toilet seat again, feeling sad and depressed.

"This is the problem with humour," he said, forlornly. "There's a cultural divide. An age divide. An individual personality divide. Everybody has a unique sense of humour. Already I'm beginning to wonder if a thirteen part treatise can do justice to such an immense and complex subject as laughter."

"You're thinking of expanding your treatise to fourteen parts?" asked Elvis.

"This is no time for sarcasm," warned Flowers.

"What is it time for?"

But before the Fat Professor could respond to the impertinence of youth, another idea had occurred to the young genius. "We need a common thread: something that will unite everybody in laughter. We need an idea that will make everybody on Earth and Stone laugh together. With that much energy we can't fail."

"I would agree with the last part," said the Fat Professor. "But you're talking pie in the sky. If we can't find a joke that the three of us can get on with, what chance is there of finding one that two entire worlds can laugh at?"

Elvis walked over to the toilet and, without a word of explanation, he flushed the chain, causing Flowers to leap off the seat for all he was worth.

"Steady," he shouted. "What do you think you're playing at?"

"I'm showing you the solution. Toilet humour – it never fails. It's what everybody has in common, here and on Stone. We've tried to be too clever. It's one of the occupational hazards of being philosophers. Don't you see?"

"See what? I'm rapidly losing patience."

"We're constipated. We need to laugh but can't. The world needs to laugh – both our worlds need the medicine of laughter. Then we can flush all the toxic waste that builds up inside us everyday – flush it down the pan, literally, and become free to fly to wherever we choose as our destination."

"To Stone?" asked the Fat Professor.

"To Stone!" said Elvis.

The philosophers looked over at the Mexican scientist, who was sobbing in the corner of the bathroom.

"What is it?" asked Elvis.

"It's beautiful," said the scientist. "It's like the fairy tales my mother used to tell me when I was child. There was always something golden in those stories, though I don't ever remember there being a golden toilet. But I think everybody in this world could relate to that idea. I think it could work."

Walton Flowers looked unconvinced. "But ... it's making you cry, man, and we want laughter."

"Don't you see?" said the scientist. "That's the twist. We tell the world about the golden toilet, a fairy tale for our times, and then we bring it down to the level of toilet humour as we *flush* the philosophers back to their world."

"Sounds like a barrel of laughs!" snorted the Fat Professor.

"Exactly," said the scientist.

"I think it will work," said Elvis. "And what have we got to lose? If we channel the energy at a mutually co-ordinated time, from here and Stone, two worlds focusing on this single golden toilet bowl ... we have to try it. Don't you see – it's our last hope."

*

And so the stage was set. Broadcasts around two worlds were to commence at midnight, GMT. The Academy working in secret, as Theodore Dee was hardly likely to endorse such an outrage.

As the hour arrived the three huddled around the golden toilet bowl and listened to the broadcast. It was the story of the Fat Professor, the philosopher genius Elvis, and the Mexican scientist trying to create enough energy through laughter to flush them though the Plato Portal that connected Earth and Stone.

The broadcaster could scarcely keep the laughter out of his voice as the ridiculous fairy tale built towards its climax.

Walton Flowers had his hand poised on the flusher, ready to deliver the punch line, when the bad news came.

There was a message from Stone. Theodore Dee had unearthed the plot and terminated the broadcast. Stone wasn't laughing anymore and likely never would again.

"It's all down to Earth now," said Elvis. "Let's hope there's enough energy here."

But the news from Stone had dampened spirits in the Fat Professor's bathroom, and the tale was almost told.

Then the scientist, listening to reports on laughter progress through the nations, chirped up. "There are reports of large-scale laughs in South America. The Mexicans, particularly, are apparently laughing in their thousands."

"They'll laugh at anything down there!" snapped Flowers, frustrated still at the news from Stone.

"The whole of America is now laughing," said the scientist. "They're laughing in Asia and … wait a minute … the Chinese have become hysterical. Australia has ground to a halt. They're laughing in Africa."

"What about Europe?" asked Elvis.

The scientist hesitated, pressed the earpiece deep into his auditory canal. "Yes! They're laughing all over Europe. Britain is laughing. London … is laughing."

The tale was ending and the Fat Professor was still brooding on Theodore Dee.

"The chain," said Elvis. "Get your hand on the chain, ready to flush."

"I can't do it," said Flowers. "I don't feel in the least … *amused*."

The tale reached its final, climactic twist.

… And as the Fat Professor, Elvis and the Mexican scientist huddled around the Golden Toilet Bowl, news came from another world … that Stone had lost the gift of laughter.

"Flush!" screamed Elvis.

"I can't," said the Fat Professor. "I can't do it … I can't go … I'm empty … there's nothing to flush."

"An unproductive flush would be useless," said the scientist. "It's just the way it is."

"It's over," said the Fat Professor. "I'm sorry."

"Unzip those trousers and get that fat butt over that bowl and give it your best shot," said Elvis, taking hold of the chain. "Do it for Stone. Are you a philosopher or just a constipated misery with a golden toilet bowl that could be sold and the money given to feed the poor?"

The sound of a zipper followed, and then ... *and then* ... the loudest, full-blooded breaking of wind in the history of fairy tale, split the air.

"The world is laughing," shouted the scientist as the farts rattled around the walls of the bathroom like so much artillery fire. "And what laughter! Never was there laughter like this!"

"I'm loosening," said the Fat Professor. "It's happening."

Then the scientist asked, "Are we ready to flush?"

There was an agonising pause, followed by the sound of the Fat Professor sighing, "Flush away, young Elvis, for the deed is truly done. The bowl is full. We're coming home."

9. THE BATTLE OF THE FAT PROFESSORS

Earth, ringing with laughter, came together in that sublime moment, as the toilet flushed and the *Tale of the Golden Toilet Bowl* was brought to completion. The Fat Professor saluted, Elvis prayed, and the Mexican scientist let go of his emotions in a deluge of tears.

Then a sequence of colours enveloped Elvis and Walton Flowers, and for long moments the two unlikely comrades were beyond words. As the colours faded to black, a sense of movement at terrifying speed overtook them, and for a seeming age it was all they knew.

Until at last white flashes exploded around them in the seconds before all movement and sense of movement came to a juddering halt.

Colour seeped back slowly, and the two travellers looked out on an unfamiliar, and at the same time *familiar*, landscape.

"Where are we?" said Elvis.

"What have they done?" said Walton Flowers.

"This can't be home," said Elvis.

"I fear it is. But what have they done to it? It's scarcely recognisable."

They were looking down from the Plato Portal located above the Dungeon on the Hill, and they were looking down on a ravished land. Sustained lack of laughter had sunk deep holes as far as the eye could see, and the ground looked cold and hungry. It did not take a philosopher to work out that sadness and despair ruled this world now, sucking out the goodness and replacing it with heartache and misery.

There was something moving on the horizon; something of considerable size. It was like a dark, formidable cloud, dense and full of foreboding, and it was heading towards the hill on which Elvis and the Fat Professor looked down on their desolated homeland.

"What's coming?" asked Elvis.

"Trouble," said the Fat Professor.

"A storm?"

"Oh, yes. A storm alright."

As the dark, monstrous shape came closer it began to resemble a living being, and one of truly epic, monstrous proportions.

"It can't be," said Elvis.

"Oh but I fear it is," said Walton Flowers.

"Nobody could be that … immense."

"They could. That is, if they'd fed long enough off the misery of their people. You can grow extremely fat and sometimes even extremely strong when you feed like that. And nobody, in the history of Stone, has ever fed off the misery of the people, or sucked out all the goodness of the land like Theodore Dee has done."

"He's coming for us? He knows we're here?"

"Yes, Elvis: he knows ... and he's coming."

"So what happens now?"

"We wait."

"Shouldn't we be preparing?"

"Preparing what, though, exactly? There's nothing we can do. I never imagined that things could have got so bad this fast. I never imagined that he - that anything - could have grown so *fat*."

"But there must be something we can do."

"Against the Fatness?" Flowers shook his head glumly.

"But you're fat too."

"Thank you," said Flowers, without an apparent trace of irony. "I am fat, it's true. But I don't *have* the Fatness. He *is* the Fatness."

Elvis sighed. This was getting them nowhere. And in the mean time, the dark shape that was Theodore Dee was almost upon them.

"If we're not going to fight, then we might as well have stayed on Earth."

Flowers turned to look at Elvis. "Not fight?" he said. "Who said anything about not fighting?"

The gigantic, fat shape of Theodore Dee was almost at the bottom of the hill.

"I don't understand," said Elvis.

"What precisely don't you understand?"

"You said there's nothing we can do."

"That's correct."

"But you also said we're going to fight."

"That's also correct. Actually, I never mentioned 'we'. *I* intend to fight. And your problem is ..?"

Elvis watched as Dee reached the bottom of the hill. "He'll never make it up here."

"Ah, the innocence of youth," said Flowers. "It's a pity you have to witness this. It's going to get ugly."

Elvis looked down at the gross blob at the foot of the hill. "I think it already has got ugly."

"You've seen nothing yet, my boy."

Hundreds of people were assembling themselves around Theodore Dee, and after a few moments the gigantic figure began to move up the hill.

"They can't do that!" said Elvis. "They're carrying him. They're acting like his slaves. Slavery has never existed here."

"It looks like a lot of things have changed while we've been gone."

In the moments that followed, Elvis thought about everything that had happened. "If I hadn't rebelled against you when you tried to ban laughter, none of this would have occurred."

"Very possibly not, but who can tell? These things are notoriously hard to define."

"Maybe banning laughter was the least of our problems."

"Or the start of them," said the Fat Professor. "I was wrong and that's all there is to it. But now I have to put everything right."

Theodore Dee was moving quickly up the hill, carried high by the hundreds of slaves beneath him. It was the most terrifying sight that Elvis had ever witnessed. The wrung-out landscape was depressing enough; but *this* ... it was nothing less than obscene.

Elvis was lost for words. It felt like ... it surely had to be ... the beginning of the end.

As the dictator reached the summit of the hill, Elvis realised the sheer immensity of Theodore Dee. Where Flowers assumed the shape of a diamond, Dee assumed almost no shape at all. He was a huge blob, a monster almost without form, with dark eyes partially hidden beneath endless rolls of facial fat, and a red gash that served for a hungry, slobbering mouth that appeared to constantly drip saliva.

At the summit the slaves carefully set down Theodore Dee, so that the great blob was a matter of feet from where Elvis and Flowers stood. The slaves, relieved of their load, fell gasping to the ground.

Elvis recoiled in horror. The slaves ... it was bad enough that slaves existed at all here, but these were his friends; students from the

Academy. As he looked closer at the mass of gasping, frightened, fragile shells of what had once been the brightest sparks in the firmament of Stone youth, he saw three ghosts.

George, Ryan and John lay on the ground in the shadow of the radiant Theodore Dee. They were hollowed out through fear and near-starvation. So traumatised and utterly defeated that they couldn't even smile when they saw their friend returned from exile.

Elvis spoke their names though none dared reply. Their faces etched in desolation, silently pleading.

Then Dee spoke, and it sounded like thunder growling over a broken world.

"Like what I've done with your precious Academy, do you, Flowers? Like what has become of your precious philosophers? Stone philosophers make the best slaves, it would seem. You should never have returned here. Stone is mine. I will crush you."

Walton Flowers said nothing, but in doing so he edged a few inches forward.

"What are you doing?" whispered Elvis. "How can you fight this *thing*?"

Flowers didn't answer. He was staring into the seething mass of fat stationed directly in front of him.

Elvis had never seen a look like it: it was an expression of sheer concentration, and in its own way it was almost as terrifying as the thing that Walton Flowers was staring *at*.

Minutes ticked by and the two Fat Professors failed to budge a single inch. On the surface of the situation it appeared that nothing at all was happening. And yet, as Elvis continued to watch, his perceptions sharpened by the tension crackling in the very air around him, he saw that underneath the apparent lack of activity, a great and profound battle was underway.

A moment of great historic significance for Stone was unfolding, and Elvis grasped the gravity of it. The Fat Professors were engaged in a staring match the like of which Stone had never seen and would likely never see again; a staring match that would be talked about as long as life itself existed on the planet.

As the battle raged, neither of the Fat Professors batted a single eye. It was looking to be a stalemate that might last for days. Weeks, even.

Then something started to happen, though at first it remained subtle and elusive. A look of uncertainty was creeping like a dark shadow across the face of Walton Flowers; and a look of quiet victory was at the same time crawling across the slobbering face of Theodore Dee.

"Do something," urged Elvis, fearing that the day was slipping towards an evil outcome.

"Any suggestions?" said Flowers out of the corner of his mouth.

"Only one," said Elvis.

"Well, make it a good one."

"Laughter," said Elvis. "That's all we've got. And it can be deadly."

Flowers, still staring at Dee, laughed. But it was a bitter, sarcastic laugh, lacking in energy and humour.

"Not you," said Elvis. "Him! We've got to make *him* laugh."

"Any suggestions on how that might be achieved? I mean to say, I don't wish to be difficult about this – but how do you propose making something as grotesque as Theodore Dee laugh?"

Elvis thought for a moment. "We need a killing joke," he said at last.

"A *what?*"

"A joke so funny that nothing and no-one, no matter how monstrous, can resist it."

"I see," said Flowers. "And this *killing joke* – I take it you have it to hand."

Elvis had heard the joke on Earth. It had been a secret weapon in the event of the laughter dens being raided, and intended for use on Walton Flowers himself.

How fitting, thought Elvis: that this joke should now be the Fat Professor's weapon in the fight against an even *fatter* professor.

It was an odd thing, this killing joke. The joke had been developed exclusively for use on adults, and intended solely for that target. It had been shown to be not the slightest bit funny when used on people under the age of sixteen. It might bring a pleasant smile to the face of a seventeen or eighteen year old with excessive maturity; but it was lost entirely on the likes of Elvis. Children, and even early to mid teenagers, were immune to certain kinds of adult humour, it seemed; and yet this joke, fully tested on adults, was known to be lethal.

A curious universe, Elvis reflected.

The joke had to be delivered by an adult; and the manner of delivery crucial to the outcome. Would it prove universal, as effective here on Stone as on Earth?

He whispered the joke into the ear of Walton Flowers, and waited.

Nothing was happening.

No, that wasn't entirely true. The intensity of Dee's stare was sucking the energy out of Walton Flowers, filling him instead with a deepening, darkening gloom; Flowers was wilting by the second.

He possessed the killing joke, yet appeared powerless to deploy.

"It's no good," he said at last. "I can't deliver your joke, Elvis. I'm just too *miserable.*"

Then Flowers' expression appeared to brighten, as though acknowledgment of his miserable state had lifted him by a fraction.

"But you've given me an idea, young Elvis," he said, his voice quickening, "and a fine one at that. Remember when I assembled you all in the Great Hall? When I set up that banana skin pratfall and nobody laughed? Remember your stroke of genius that day?"

Of course Elvis remembered it. And he said as much, observing the gloom sliding now off the face of Walton Flowers, and a hint of light cutting like a sword through the darkness.

Flowers stepped forward.

The silence was thunderous, but the sound that followed it was shocking. It was like a voice from a grave, a ripping, tearing sound. A sound that conjured sewers, evoking an accompanying smell that was worse than a thousand corpses rotting out in the heat of the day.

Yet where was the sound coming from? The slaves were not daring to move a muscle. And the mouths of both the Fat Professors were tightly closed.

Then it came again, that vile sound.

Elvis felt his nostrils twitching. The sound was doing more than conjuring up that dreadful smell – the smell was real. The smell was accompanying the sound, appearing to the nasal sense a mere second or so after its preceding sound had reached the ears.

He covered his face against the terrible smell.

And then he realised what was happening.

The sound … it was a passage from Plato, but spoken, not through the mouth – but through … the portal below.

Walton Flowers' backside was quoting Plato!

"Oh, yes," said Flowers. "I was inspired by your great statement of intent in the Great Hall on the day I tried to ban laughter; but I can go one better. I have practised for this, young Elvis. I have practised for many long hours, coached in the art by London's finest. Call me a hypocrite – but you'll forgive me when you see what I can achieve here today. So lend me your ears, your eyes, your nostrils, and see what I can do."

Elvis, slightly confused by this last utterance, nevertheless lent both his eyes along with both ears and his twitching nostrils, and found that his generosity was well rewarded.

Out of the stillness it came again, this time a famous passage from '*The Republic*', followed by a passage from '*The Death of Socrates*'. One classic after another; Flowers was on fire – his backside at least.

This by any standards was a formidable performance, sheer virtuosity. The slaves, against all the rules, were cracking at last, returning to life and liberty, their ribs aching with laughter.

But somehow, against all the rules of logic, Theodore Dee was holding out.

"Silence!" he thundered. "Another slave laughs and I'll have him thrown off this hill to the vultures circling below. And what's more I'll have his family rounded up and fed to the vultures too."

The laughter abruptly ended. But Walton Flowers was far from finished. A tremendous sound issued from the back of his trousers, in answer to Theodore Dee. It was a sound containing the essence of the great Plato himself in all his Stone-born glory.

"Go for it!" yelled Elvis, thrilled by the magnificence of his teacher's amazing display. "No-one can resist this."

But Dee was resisting.

Dee wasn't so much as cracking a smile. A selection from every single masterpiece of Plato, all delivered so clearly that you couldn't mistake a syllable, and still the monstrous blob refused to laugh.

Walton Flowers, climaxing with a show-stopping selection from the lesser known works of Greek legend, stopped at last, clearly exhausted by his monumental efforts. "It's no good," he said. "Even genius cannot win a day like this. I fear that we are defeated."

Elvis groaned. It was not merely the prospect of defeat and all that entailed; it was the fact that Flowers had that pompous tone back in his voice. A sermon was coming. As if things weren't bad enough, he was going to deliver, even now, a lecture on the subject.

"… And on this day Stone falls into its Dark Age. Today philosophy itself stands defeated. This day of days is written on the wind that doesn't stir, and in the molecules of space that swim throughout the universe in morbid self-pity. This abominable day when wretches walk the stars above us and drab grey becomes the colour of space itself …"

Elvis couldn't bear it. He covered his ears against the unendurable rubbish spewing out of the hole in the Fat Professor's face. Yet despite his hands being pressed firmly against his ears, a sound leaked through that had no place in this appalling moment.

The sound of … it couldn't be … surely not …*could it?*

Theodore Dee was quivering, shaking as though an uncontrollable spasm had seized him. And that sound – at the same time hideous and pure delight.

"He's – he's laughing!" screamed Elvis. "I don't believe it! He's really laughing."

"Have I said something amusing?" said Flowers, utterly bemused.

"I said you were funniest when you were being miserable and serious."

Without intending to, Walton Flowers broke wind. It was a savage, merciless delivery of all that remained inside him; and in his now weakened state, Theodore Dee could not resist it, collapsing to the ground, laughing so hard that he was begging for mercy.

But Flowers was looking down on the bellowing mass of gyrating fatness and clearly intending to show no mercy. "Want some more Plato, do you?"

And so the Fat Professor gave his encore. Extended highlights from his earlier repertoire. The best of Plato, quoted from no less a sacred place than the seat of the trousers. He was digging deep, exploring reserves that he never knew he had.

Flowers didn't stop until Dee was finished, and a final quote from *The Death of Socrates* served as both eulogy and fitting end to the most savage chapter in Stone's history.

The slaves, joyful in their release from bondage, carried the lifeless body of Theodore Dee to the edge of the hill and unceremoniously flung him to the waiting vultures.

10. A NEW DAWN

An urgent meeting was called in the Great Hall.

Walton Flowers took to the stage.

This time there were no banana skins.

"… And so in my time of exile I discovered that responsibility and fun, laughter and philosophy, can live together. The age of extremes is over; there is a *Middle Way*. There is … *A Philosophy of Laughter*."

Indeed there was. And copies of the book were on sale at the back of the hall.

In the dormitories of the Academy, after lights out, Elvis sat holding a copy of the Fat Professor's book. George, Ryan and John sat opposite. They looked a lot better these days, light and joyful and full of fun; back to their old selves, thought Elvis.

"This book," he said, "is meant to be deadly serious."

"You're not kidding," said George.

"A laugh a minute," said Ryan.

"A veritable hoot," said John.

"Exactly," said Elvis. "It's the funniest book ever written. Getting rid of Dee stopped things from getting any worse, but the laughs in this book are bringing Stone back to life. Flowers has changed in almost every possible way. But in one way he hasn't changed at all. When he tries to be serious, he's still the funniest guy in the universe."

"Are you getting a commission for saying things like that?" asked George.

"Just read the book," said Elvis. "You'll see I'm telling the truth."

"You're really not getting paid for this?" asked Ryan.

"You don't trust me?"

"We trust you," said John. "Of course we trust you. It's just that ..."

"No," said Elvis. "You either trust me or you don't. Either/Or. What's it to be?"

His three best friends looked at each other. George was first to break out in a grin, but the others weren't more than a second behind.

"We trust you," they said in chorus.

*

Elvis went outside. It was a clear night and the stars looked immaculate in the black sky. He thought of his time on Earth and of the changes that had taken place there and here. He thought of what the future might hold for Stone: for his friends at the Academy; for his family out in the far-off country.

At last he went back inside.

There was a lot of noise coming from the dormitory. As Elvis went in he saw George, Ryan and John, rolling around on the floor like they were having a violent fit in triplicate. He was about to call for help when he noticed the Fat Professor's book open on one of the beds.

"Been reading have you boys?"

But his friends were laughing so hard that all they could do was hold their aching sides and concentrate on trying to breathe.

"I think you've overdone it for tonight. More than two pages of that stuff and you're going to make yourselves ill."

*

As Stone grew back to life, with Walton Flowers leading the mission to restore the planet to its former glories, and fully implement his radical new philosophy, the time came to call one more meeting in the Great Hall.

"As you all know," said Flowers from the stage, "laughter is a serious business. We are making progress but I cannot work miracles single-handed. And so, today, I am announcing, without further ado, that I intend, without further hesitation, to appoint an understudy to assist me. So, it is with great pleasure, that I invite Elvis to come up onto the stage to formally accept the new position of Under-Professor."

To great applause Elvis made his way to the front of the hall and up the steps, where he joined the Fat Professor under the spotlight.

With great ceremony Walton Flowers picked up a large, gold chain and approached his newly appointed assistant.

"No," said Elvis.

The crowd gasped.

"There is," said Elvis, "a condition."

"Condition?" said Flowers.

"If I accept this position it is on the condition that all Academy students are re-united with their families for at least part of the year."

The hall descended into a ponderous hush. Nobody moved a muscle. Then Flowers, turning away from Elvis, moved to the front of the stage and took hold of the microphone.

"Condition ... *accepted*."

*

At the end of term Elvis was busy packing his rucksack when George came into the dormitory.

"How are you feeling?" said Elvis.

"I'm a little nervous, to tell you the truth. I haven't seen my family for so long I can't even remember what they look like."

Then Ryan came in.

"Are you nervous too?" asked Elvis.

Ryan nodded.

Finally John came in, sitting on his bed, looking like he was about to cry.

"Listen," said Elvis. "We're all going our separate ways, but we'll be back at the start of next term. Your folks will be as nervous as you are. But you'll all have adventures together, things you can't even imagine, and things will work out because Stone's changed. It will never be so bad again."

Then he turned to his bedside cabinet. "Oops, almost forgot."

From the cabinet he took out a well-read copy of the Fat Professor's book and stuffed it into his rucksack before fastening it up. "The perfect holiday read. Just in case things get, you know … and I need the medicine of a good laugh. Pack yourselves a copy and see you in a few weeks."

He watched as his friends' faces lit, one by one, and then he gestured to them to come together. And standing in a small circle, Elvis recited from Walton Flowers' book until the four of them could hardly stand for laughing.

*

Elvis left as a new dawn was breaking over the Academy and over Stone. There was no need for goodbyes, and the Fat Professor's book felt as light as a smile in his rucksack.

He set off for the far country without looking back.

THE END

Printed in Great Britain
by Amazon